MARC BROWN

ARTHUR LOST AND FOUND

RED FOX

For Sunny Macmillan,
with many thanks

A Red Fox Book

Published by Random House Children's Books
20 Vauxhall Bridge Road, London SW1V 2SA

A division of Random House UK Ltd
London Melbourne Sydney Auckland
Johannesburg and agencies throughout the world

Copyright © 1998 Marc Brown

1 3 5 7 9 10 8 6 4 2

First published in the United States of America by
Little, Brown & Company and simultaneously in Canada by
Little, Brown & Company (Canada) Ltd 1998

First published in Great Britain by Red Fox 1999

Printed in Hong Kong.

RANDOM HOUSE UK Limited Reg. No. 954009

ISBN 0 09 940395 1

"What are you supposed to be?" asked Arthur.
"I'm mashed potatoes," said D.W., "in the Festival of Foods at school tomorrow."

"I've got to go to my swimming lesson," said Arthur.
"You'll have to take the bus to your lesson," said his
mother, "and I'll pick you up."
"All by myself?" asked Arthur.

"We've taken the bus before," she said. "You know how."

"Maybe I'll ask Buster to come along," said Arthur.

"Good idea," agreed his mother.

On the way to school, Arthur invited Buster.
"You mean the real bus?" asked Buster. "The one that goes all the way to the end of town?"
"Yes," said Arthur. "We just pay our money and go."

"I don't know," said Buster. "I heard about this man who got on the bus, and it just kept going and going and going."

"We can study for our science test, and you can watch me swim," said Arthur. "It'll be fun."

After school, Arthur and Buster waited at the bus stop.
"Did you hear about the boy who didn't have enough
money?" asked Francine. "The driver wouldn't let him
off the bus."
All of a sudden Arthur didn't feel very well.
"Here comes the bus!" said Francine. "Good luck."

BUS STOP

ITY MAP

ELWOOD CITY

LOSE PO
THE FUN
WAY!

DIET
PLAYGROUND

TOLON

MAIL

"Exact change only," growled the driver
The boys paid him and quickly took their seats.
"Want to study for the test?" asked Arthur.
"Not really," said Buster.
Arthur took out his science book.
" 'Chapter six,' " read Arthur. " 'Habits of the Clam . . .' "

By the time the bus stopped at the swimming pool,
Arthur and Buster were sound asleep.
"Last stop," called the driver. "Everyone out!"
"Where are we?" asked Arthur.
"Who knows?" said Buster. "I think we passed the pool."

"I've never seen this side of town before," said Buster.
"We're lost!"
"Maybe we can find a policeman," said Arthur.

"Wait!" said Arthur. "There's a place with a phone!"

Homemade fresh Pie!

Pancake Special

But the telephone had a sign on it.
"Sorry, it's been broken for weeks," said the man behind
the counter.

"I'm hungry," said Buster. "I always get hungry when I'm scared."

"No, you're just always hungry," said Arthur.

They bought some chocolate and two cans of fizzy strawberry drink and thought about what to do next.

Meanwhile, back at home, the phone rang.

Arthur's little sister ran to answer it.

"Mom," D.W. yelled, "did we lose Arthur somewhere?"

"He's at his swimming lesson," said her mother. "In fact, it's almost time to pick him up. Who is it?"

"It's the man from the pool," said D.W. "Arthur isn't there."

"Give me the phone," gasped her mother. "What do you mean he's not there?"

"If Arthur's lost," said D.W., "can I have his room?"

Arthur and Buster finished their snacks. Then Arthur had an idea.

"Let's go back to the bus stop and try and get a bus home," said Arthur.

"Great idea!" said Buster. "Can you lend me some money for the bus? I spent all my money on chocolate."

"Sure," said Arthur.

But when Arthur reached into his pocket, it was empty.

"Oh, no," said Arthur. "I spent all my money on drinks!"

"We're doomed," said Buster.

"Let's go to the bus stop anyway," said Arthur. "Maybe we can talk to the bus driver."

ELWOOD CITY LIBRARY
READATHON WEEK

Arthur and Buster raced to the bus stop.
The bus was just pulling away.
"Oh, no!" said Arthur. "Wait! WAIT!" he called.
The bus squealed to a stop.

"Whaddaya kids want?" asked the driver.
"We're lost," Arthur explained. "We were supposed to get off at the swimming pool, but we fell asleep and then we spent all our money on chocolate. Now we can't get home, and I'm really sorry."
"Hey, kids," said the driver, "I've heard enough. Happens all the time."
"Really?" asked Arthur.

PEACE TALKS

"Hop on," said the driver. "By the way, my name's Sam."
"I'm Arthur. He's Buster."
"Let's make a quick stop and give your parents a call,"
said Sam. "Just in case they're getting a little nervous."
"Great idea," said Arthur.

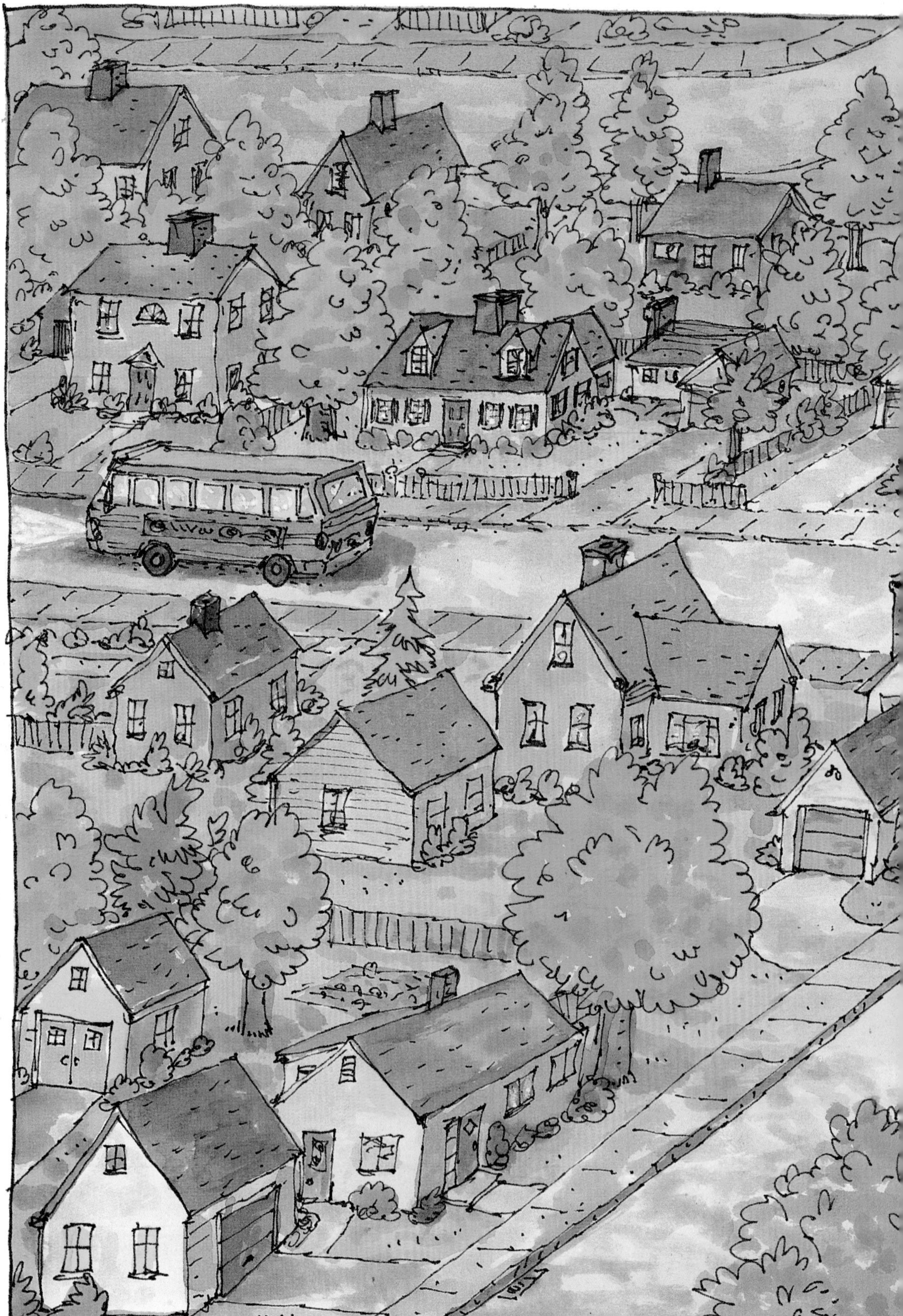

Sam stopped the bus right in front of
Arthur's house instead of at the corner.
"Thanks, Sam," said Arthur and Buster.
"See ya 'round," said Sam.
Everyone on the bus waved goodbye.

When Arthur opened the door, his family ran to give him
kisses and hugs.
D.W. was so happy that she hugged Buster, too.
"No kisses, please," said Buster.
Arthur told his family everything that had happened.

"I liked the part where you were lost best," said D.W.
"That's when I had a new bedroom."
Then Dad gave Buster a lift home.

That night, when his parents tucked Arthur into bed,
he was very sleepy.
"You were very clever to work out what to do," said his mother.
"We're very proud of you," said his father.
They kissed Arthur good night and turned off the light.

Suddenly, the door burst open and the light came on.
"What's going on?" said Arthur.
"I'm making sure you're not lost again," said D.W.
"Good brothers are hard to find."
Arthur yawned. "So are good sisters.
Good night, D.W."